THE TAILOR OF GLOSTER

TITTLE-MOUSE

SQUIRREL NUTKIN

NUTS

TOM KITTEN

PETER RABBIT

TO
MARGERY, JEAN
AND DAVID

FREDERICK WARNE

Published by the Penguin Group
Registered office: 80 Strand, London, WC2R ORL
Penguin Young Readers Group, 345 Hudson Street, New York, N.Y. 10014, USA

First published 1930 by Frederick Warne
This edition with new reproductions of Beatrix Potter's book illustrations first published 2007
This edition copyright © Frederick Warne & Co. 2007
New reproductions of Beatrix Potter's book illustrations copyright © Frederick Warne & Co. 2002
Original copyright in text and illustrations © Frederick Warne & Co., 1930

Manufactured in China

THE TALE OF
LITTLE PIG ROBINSON

BY BEATRIX POTTER

FREDERICK WARNE

Chapter One

WHEN I was a child I used to go to the seaside
for the holidays. We stayed in a little town where
there was a harbour and fishing boats and fishermen.
They sailed away to catch herrings in nets. When the
boats came back home again some had only caught
a few herrings. Others had caught so many that
they could not all be unloaded on to the quay.
Then horses and carts were driven into the shallow
water at low tide to meet the heavily laden boats.
The fish were shovelled over the side of the boat
into the carts, and taken to the railway station,
where a special train of fish trucks was waiting.

Great was the excitement when the fishing
boats returned with a good catch of herrings.
Half the people in the town ran down to the
quay, including cats.

THERE was a white cat called Susan who never missed meeting the boats. She belonged to the wife of an old fisherman named Sam. The wife's name was Betsy. She had rheumatics, and she had no family except Susan and five hens. Betsy sat by the fire; her back ached; she said "Ow! Ow!" whenever she had to put coal on, and stir the pot.

SUSAN sat opposite to Betsy. She felt sorry for Betsy; she wished she knew how to put the coal on and stir the pot. All day long they sat by the fire, while Sam was away fishing. They had a cup of tea and some milk.

"Susan," said Betsy, "I can hardly stand up. Go to the front gate and look out for Master's boat."

Susan went out and came back. Three or four times she went out into the garden. At last, late in the afternoon, she saw the sails of the fishing fleet, coming in over the sea.

"Go down to the harbour; ask Master for six herrings; I will cook them for supper. Take my basket, Susan."

Susan took the basket; also she borrowed Betsy's bonnet and little plaid shawl. I saw her hurrying down to the harbour.

OTHER cats were coming out of the cottages, and running down the steep streets that lead to the sea front. Also ducks. I remember that they were most peculiar ducks with top-knots that looked like tam-o'-shanter caps. Everybody was hurrying to meet the boats — nearly everybody. I only met one person, a dog called Stumpy, who was going the opposite way. He was carrying a paper parcel in his mouth.

SOME dogs do not care for fish. Stumpy had been to the butcher's to buy mutton chops for himself and Bob and Percy and Miss Rose. Stumpy was a large, serious, well-behaved brown dog with a short tail. He lived with Bob the retriever and Percy the cat and Miss Rose who kept house. Stumpy had belonged to a very rich old gentleman; and when the old gentleman died he left money to Stumpy — ten shillings a week for the rest of Stumpy's life. So that was why Stumpy and Bob and Percy the cat all lived together in a pretty little house.

Susan with her basket met Stumpy at the corner of Broad Street. Susan made a curtsy. She would have stopped to inquire after Percy, only she was in a hurry to meet the boat. Percy was lame; he had hurt his foot. It had been trapped under the wheel of a milk cart.

Stumpy looked at Susan out of the corner of his eye; he wagged his tail, but he did not stop.

HE could not bow or say "good afternoon" for fear of dropping the parcel of mutton chops. He turned out of Broad Street into Woodbine Lane, where he lived; he pushed open the front door

and disappeared into a house. Presently there was a smell of cooking, and I have no doubt that Stumpy and Bob and Miss Rose enjoyed their mutton chops.

Percy could not be found at dinner-time. He had slipped out of the window, and, like all the other cats in the town, he had gone to meet the fishing boats.

SUSAN hurried along Broad Street and took
the short cut to the harbour, down a steep flight
of steps. The ducks had wisely gone another way,
round by the sea front. The steps were too steep
and slippery for anyone less sure-footed than a cat.
Susan went down quickly and easily. There were
forty-three steps, rather dark and slimy, between
high backs of houses.

A smell of ropes and pitch and a good deal of
noise came up from below. At the bottom of the
steps was the quay, or landing place, beside the
inner harbour.

The tide was out; there was no water; the vessels
rested on the dirty mud. Several ships were
moored beside the quay; others were anchored
inside the breakwater.

NEAR the steps, coal was being unloaded from
two grimy colliers called the "Margery Dawe" of
Sunderland, and the "Jenny Jones" of Cardiff. Men
ran along planks with wheelbarrowfuls of coal;
coal scoops were swung ashore by cranes, and
emptied with loud thumping and rattling.

Farther along the quay, another ship called the
"Pound of Candles" was taking a mixed cargo on
board. Bales, casks, packing-cases, barrels — all
manner of goods were being stowed into the hold;
sailors and stevedores shouted; chains rattled
and clanked. Susan waited for an opportunity
to slip past the noisy crowd. She watched a cask
of cider that bobbed and swung in the air, on its
passage from the quay to the deck of the "Pound
of Candles".

A yellow cat who sat in the rigging was also watching the cask.

The rope ran through the pulley; the cask went down bobbitty on to the deck, where a sailor man was waiting for it. Said the sailor down below:

"Look out! Mind your head, young sir! Stand out of the way!"

"Wee, wee, wee!" grunted a small pink pig, scampering round the deck of the "Pound of Candles".

The yellow cat in the rigging watched the small pink pig. The yellow cat in the rigging looked across at Susan on the quay. The yellow cat winked.

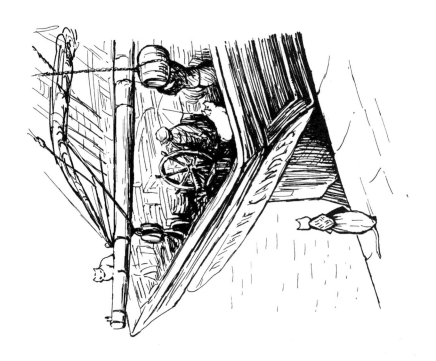

SUSAN was surprised to see a pig on board a ship. But she was in a hurry. She threaded her way along the quay, amongst coal and cranes, and men wheeling hand-trucks, and noises, and smells. She passed the fish auction, and fish boxes, and fish sorters, and barrels that women were filling with herrings and salt.

Seagulls swooped and screamed. Hundreds of fish boxes and tons of fresh fish were being loaded into the hold of a small steamer. Susan was glad to get away from the crowd, down a much shorter flight of steps on to the shore of the outer harbour. The ducks arrived soon afterwards, waddling and quacking. And old Sam's boat, the "Betsy Timmins", last of the herring fleet and heavy laden, came in round the breakwater; and drove her blunt nose into the shingle.

SAM was in high spirits; he had had a big catch. He and his mate and two lads commenced to unload their fish into carts, as the tide was too low to float the fishing boat up to the quay. The boat was full of herrings.

But, good luck or bad luck, Sam never failed to throw a handful of herrings to Susan.

"Here's for the two old girls and a hot supper! Catch them, Susan! Honest now! Here's a broken fish for you! Now take the others to Betsy."

The ducks were dabbling and gobbling; the seagulls were screaming and swooping. Susan climbed the steps with her basket of herrings and went home by back streets.

Old Betsy cooked two herrings for herself and Susan, another two for Sam's supper when he came in. Then she went to bed with a hot bottle wrapped in a flannel petticoat to help her rheumatics.

SAM ate his supper and smoked a pipe by the fire; and then he went to bed. But Susan sat a long time by the fire, considering. She considered many things — fish, and ducks, and Percy with a lame foot, and dogs that eat mutton chops, and the yellow cat on the ship, and the pig. Susan thought it strange to see a pig upon a ship called the "Pound of Candles". The mice peeped out under the cupboard door. The cinders fell together on the hearth. Susan purred gently in her sleep and dreamed of fish and pigs. She could not understand that pig on board a ship. But I know all about him!

Chapter Two

YOU remember the song about the Owl and the Pussy Cat and their beautiful pea-green boat? How they took some honey and plenty of money, wrapped up in a five pound note?

They sailed away, for a year and a day,
To the land where the Bong tree grows —
And, there in a wood, a piggy-wig stood,
With a ring at the end of his nose — his nose,
With a ring at the end of his nose.

Now I am going to tell you the story of that pig, and why he went to live in the land of the Bong tree.

WHEN that pig was little he lived in
Devonshire, with his aunts, Miss Dorcas and Miss
Porcas, at a farm called Piggery Porcombe. Their
cosy thatched cottage was in an orchard at the top
of a steep red Devonshire lane.

The soil was red, the grass was green; and far away
below in the distance they could see red cliffs and a
bit of bright blue sea. Ships with white sails sailed
over the sea into the harbour of Stymouth.

I have often remarked that the Devonshire
farms have very strange names. If you had ever
seen Piggery Porcombe you would think that the
people who lived there were very queer too! Aunt
Dorcas was a stout speckled pig who kept hens.

AUNT PORCAS was a large smiling black pig who took in washing. We shall not hear very much about them in this story. They led prosperous uneventful lives, and their end was bacon. But their nephew Robinson had the most peculiar adventures that ever happened to a pig.

Little pig Robinson was a charming little fellow; pinky white with small blue eyes, fat cheeks and a double chin, and a turned-up nose, with a real silver ring in it. Robinson could see that ring if he shut one eye and squinted sideways.

He was always contented and happy. All day long he ran about the farm, singing little songs to himself, and grunting "Wee, wee, wee!" His aunts missed those little songs sadly after Robinson had left them.

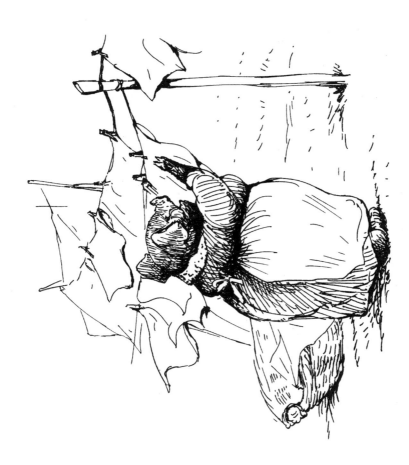

23

"WEE? Wee? Wee?" he answered when anybody spoke to him. "Wee? Wee? Wee?" listening with his head on one side and one eye screwed up.

Robinson's old aunts fed him and petted him and kept him on the trot.

"Robinson! Robinson!" called Aunt Dorcas. "Come quick! I hear a hen clucking. Fetch me the egg; don't break it now!"

"Wee, wee, wee!" answered Robinson, like a little Frenchman.

"Robinson! Robinson! I've dropped a clothes peg, come and pick it up for me!" called Aunt Porcas from the drying green (she being almost too fat to stoop down and pick up anything).

"Wee, wee, wee!" answered Robinson.

BOTH the aunts were very, very stout. And
the stiles in the neighbourhood of Stymouth are
narrow. The footpath from Piggery Porcombe
crosses many fields; a red trodden track between
short green grass and daisies. And wherever the
footpath crosses over from one field to another
field, there is sure to be a stile in the hedge.

"It is not me that is too stout; it is the stiles that
are too thin," said Aunt Dorcas to Aunt Porcas.
"Could you manage to squeeze through them if
I stayed at home?"

"I could *not*. Not for two years I could *not*," replied
Aunt Porcas. "Aggravating, it *is* aggravating of that
carrier man, to go and upset his donkey cart the day
before market day. And eggs at two and tuppence
a dozen! How far do you call it to walk all the way
round by the road instead of crossing the fields?"

"FOUR miles if it's one," sighed Aunt Porcas, "and me using my last bit of soap. However will we get our shopping done? The donkey says the cart will take a week to mend."

"Don't you think you could squeeze through the stiles if you went before dinner?"

"No, I don't, I would stick fast; and so would you," said Aunt Porcas.

"Don't you think we might venture —" commenced Aunt Dorcas.

"Venture to send Robinson by the footpath to Stymouth?" finished Aunt Porcas.

"Wee, wee, wee!" answered Robinson.

"I scarcely like to send him alone, though he is sensible for his size."

"Wee, wee, wee!" answered Robinson.

"But there is nothing else to be done," said Aunt Dorcas.

SO Robinson was popped into the wash-tub with the last bit of soap. He was scrubbed and dried and polished as bright as a new pin. Then he was dressed in a little blue cotton frock and knickers, and instructed to go shopping to Stymouth with a big market basket.

In the basket were two dozen eggs, a bunch of daffodils, two spring cauliflowers; also Robinson's dinner of bread-and-jam sandwiches. The eggs and flowers and vegetables he must sell in the market, and bring back various other purchases from shopping.

"NOW take care of yourself in Stymouth, Nephew Robinson. Beware of gunpowder, and ships' cooks, and pantechnicons, and sausages, and shoes, and ships, and sealing-wax. Remember the blue bag, the soap, the darning wool — what was the other thing?" said Aunt Dorcas.

"The darning wool, the soap, the blue bag, the yeast — what was the other thing?" said Aunt Porcas.

"Wee, wee, wee!" answered Robinson.

"The blue bag, the soap, the yeast, the darning wool, the cabbage seed — that's five, and there ought to be six. It was two more than four because it was two too many to tie knots in the corners of his hankie, to remember by. Six to buy, it should be —"

"I have it!" said Aunt Porcas. "It was tea — tea, blue bag, soap, darning wool, yeast, cabbage seed. You will buy most of them at Mr. Mumby's. Explain about the carrier, Robinson; tell him we will bring the washing and some more vegetables next week."

"Wee, wee, wee!" answered Robinson, setting off with the big basket.

AUNT DORCAS and Aunt Porcas stood in the porch. They watched him safely out of sight, down the field, and through the first of the many stiles. When they went back to their household tasks they were grunty and snappy with each other, because they were uneasy about Robinson.

"I wish we had not let him go. You and your tiresome blue bag!" said Aunt Dorcas.

"Blue bag, indeed! It was your darning wool and eggs!" grumbled Aunt Porcas. "Bother that carrier man and his donkey cart! Why could not he keep out of the ditch until after market day?"

Chapter Three

THE walk to Stymouth was a long one, in spite
of going by the fields. But the footpath ran
downhill all the way, and Robinson was merry. He
sang his little song, for joy of the fine morning, and
he chuckled "Wee, wee, wee!" Larks were singing,
too, high overhead.

And higher still — high up against blue sky,
the great white gulls sailed in wide circles. Their
hoarse cries came softened back to earth from a
great way up above. Important rooks and lively
jackdaws strutted about the meadows amongst the
daisies and buttercups. Lambs skipped and baa'ed;
the sheep looked round at Robinson.

"Mind yourself in Stymouth, little pig," said a
motherly ewe.

ROBINSON trotted on until he was out of breath and very hot. He had crossed five big fields, and ever so many stiles; stiles with steps; ladder stiles; stiles of wooden posts; some of them were very awkward with a heavy basket. The farm of Piggery Porcombe was no longer in sight when he looked back. In the distance before him, beyond the farmlands and cliffs — never any nearer — the dark blue sea rose like a wall.

Robinson sat down to rest beside a hedge in a sheltered sunny spot. Yellow pussy willow catkins were in flower above his head; there were primroses in hundreds on the bank, and a warm smell of moss and grass and steaming moist red earth.

"IF I eat my dinner now, I will not have to carry it. Wee, wee, wee!" said Robinson.

The walk had made him so hungry he would have liked to eat an egg as well as the jam sandwiches; but he had been too well brought up.

"It would spoil the two dozen," said Robinson.

He picked a bunch of primroses and tied them up with a bit of darning wool that Aunt Dorcas had given him for a pattern.

"I will sell them in the market for my very own self, and buy sweeties with my pennies. How many pennies have I got?" said Robinson, feeling in his pocket. "One from Aunt Dorcas, and one from Aunt Porcas, and one for my primroses for my very own self — oh, wee, wee, wee! There is somebody trotting along the road! I shall be late for market!"

ROBINSON jumped up and pushed his basket through a very narrow stile, where the footpath crossed into the public road. He saw a man on horseback. Old Mr. Pepperil came up, riding a chestnut horse with white legs. His two tall greyhounds ran before him; they looked through the bars of the gates into every field that they passed. They came bounding up to Robinson, very large and friendly; they licked his face and asked what he had got in that basket. Mr. Pepperil called them.

"Here, Pirate! Here, Postboy! Come here, sir!" He did not wish to be answerable for the eggs.

THE road had been recently covered with sharp new flints. Mr. Pepperil walked the chestnut horse on the grass edge, and talked to Robinson. He was a jolly old gentleman, very affable, with a red face and white whiskers. All the green fields and red ploughland between Stymouth and Piggery Porcombe belonged to him.

"Hullo, hullo! And where are you off to, little pig Robinson?"

"Please, Mr. Pepperil, sir, I'm going to market. Wee, wee, wee!" said Robinson.

"What, all by yourself? Where are Miss Dorcas and Miss Porcas? Not ill, I trust?"

Robinson explained about the narrow stiles.

"Dear, dear! Too fat, too fat? So you are going all alone? Why don't your aunts keep a dog to run errands?"

ROBINSON answered all Mr. Pepperil's questions very sensibly and prettily. He showed much intelligence, and quite a good knowledge of vegetables, for one so young. He trotted along almost under the horse, looking up at its shiny chestnut coat, and the broad white girth, and Mr. Pepperil's gaiters and brown leather boots. Mr. Pepperil was pleased with Robinson; he gave him another penny. At the end of the flints, he gathered up the reins and touched the horse with his heel.

"Well, good day, little pig. Kind regards to the aunts. Mind yourself in Stymouth." He whistled for his dogs, and trotted away.

ROBINSON continued to walk along the road. He passed by an orchard where seven thin dirty pigs were grubbing. They had no silver rings in their noses! He crossed Styford bridge without stopping to look over the parapet at the little fishes, swimming head up stream, balanced in the sluggish current; or the white ducks that dabbled amongst floating masses of water-crowsfoot. At Styford Mill he called to leave a message from Aunt Dorcas to the Miller about meal; the Miller's wife gave him an apple.

AT the house beyond the mill, there is a big dog that barks; but the big dog Gypsy only smiled and wagged his tail at Robinson. Several carts and gigs overtook him. First, two old farmers who screwed themselves round to stare at Robinson. They had two geese, a sack of potatoes, and some cabbages, sitting on the back seat of their gig. Then an old woman passed in a donkey cart with seven hens, and long pink bundles of rhubarb that had been grown in straw under apple barrels. Then with a rattle and a jingle of cans came Robinson's cousin, little Tom Pigg, driving a strawberry roan pony, in a milk float.

He might have offered Robinson a lift, only he happened to be going in the opposite direction; in fact, the strawberry roan pony was running away home.

"THIS little pig went to market!" shouted little
Tom Pigg gaily, as he rattled out of sight in a cloud
of dust, leaving Robinson standing in the road.

ROBINSON walked on along the road, and presently he came to another stile in the opposite hedge, where the footpath followed the fields again. Robinson got his basket through the stile. For the first time he felt some apprehension. In this field there were cows; big sleek Devon cattle, dark red like their native soil. The leader of the herd was a vicious old cow, with brass balls screwed on to the tips of her horns. She stared disagreeably at Robinson. He sidled across the meadow and got out through the farther stile as quickly as he could. Here the new trodden footpath followed round the edge of a crop of young green wheat. Someone let off a gun with a bang that made Robinson jump and cracked one of Aunt Dorcas's eggs in the basket.

A cloud of rooks and jackdaws rose cawing and scolding from the wheat. Other sounds mingled with their cries; noises of the town of Stymouth that began to come in sight through the elm trees that bordered the fields; distant noises from the station; whistling of an engine; the bump of trucks shunting; noise of workshops; the hum of a distant town; the hooter of a steamer entering the harbour. High overhead came the hoarse cry of the gulls, and the squabbling cawing of rooks, old and young, in their rookery up in the elm trees.

Robinson left the fields for the last time and joined a stream of country people on foot and in carts, all going to Stymouth Market.

Chapter Four

STYMOUTH is a pretty little town, situated
at the mouth of the river Pigsty, whose sluggish
waters slide gently into a bay sheltered by high
red headlands. The town itself seems to be sliding
downhill in a basin of hills, all slipping seaward
into Stymouth harbour, which is dammed back
by quays and the outer breakwater.

THE outskirts of the town are untidy, as is frequently the case with seaports. A straggling suburb on the western approach is inhabited principally by goats, and persons who deal in old iron, rags, tarred rope, and fishing nets. There are rope walks, and washing that flaps on waggling lines above banks of stony shingle, littered with seaweed, whelk shells and dead crabs — very different from Aunt Porcas's clothes lines over the clean green grass.

49

AND there are marine stores that sell spy-glasses, and sou'westers, and onions; and there are smells; and curious high sheds, shaped like sentry boxes, where they hang up herring nets to dry; and loud talking inside dirty houses. It seemed a likely place to meet a pantechnicon. Robinson kept in the middle of the road. Somebody in a public-house shouted at him through the window, "Come in, fat pig!" Robinson took to his heels.

THE town of Stymouth itself is clean, pleasant, picturesque, and well-behaved (always excepting the harbour); but it is extremely steep downhill. If Robinson had started one of Aunt Dorcas's eggs rolling at the top of High Street, it would have rolled all the way down to the bottom; only it would have got broken certainly against a doorstep, or underfoot. There were crowds in the streets, as it was market day.

INDEED, it was difficult to walk about without being pushed off the pavement; every old woman that Robinson met seemed to have a basket as big as his own. In the roadway were fish barrows, apple barrows, stalls with crockery and hardware, cocks and hens riding in pony carts, donkeys with panniers, and farmers with wagon-loads of hay. Also there was a constant string of coal carts coming up from the docks. To a country-bred pig, the noise was confusing and fearful.

53

ROBINSON kept his head very creditably until he got into Fore Street, where a drover's dog was trying to turn three bullocks into a yard, assisted by Stumpy and half the other dogs of the town. Robinson and two other little pigs with baskets of asparagus bolted down an alley and hid in a doorway until the noise of bellowing and barking had passed.

When Robinson took courage to come out again into Fore Street, he decided to follow close behind the tail of a donkey who was carrying panniers piled high with spring broccoli. There was no difficulty in guessing which road led to market. But after all these delays it was not surprising that the church clock struck eleven.

ALTHOUGH it had been open since ten, there were still plenty of customers buying, and wanting to buy, in the market hall. It was a large, airy, light, cheerful, covered-in place, with glass in the roof. It was crowded, but safe and pleasant, compared with the jostling and racket outside in the cobble-paved streets; at all events there was no risk of being run over. There was a loud hum of voices; market folk cried their wares; customers elbowed and pushed round the stalls. Dairy produce, vegetables, fish, and shell fish were displayed upon the flat boards on trestles.

Robinson had found a standing place at one end of a stall where Nanny Nettigoat was selling periwinkles.

"WINKLE, winkle! Wink, wink, wink! Maa,
maa-a!" bleated Nanny.

Winkles were the only thing that she offered
for sale, so she felt no jealousy of Robinson's
eggs and primroses. She knew nothing about his
cauliflowers; he had the sense to keep them in the
basket under the table. He stood on an empty box,
quite proud and bold behind the trestle table,
singing:

"Eggs, new laid! Fresh new-laid eggs! Who'll
come and buy my eggs and daffodillies?"

"I will, sure," said a large brown dog with a
stumpy tail, "I'll buy a dozen. My Miss Rose
has sent me to market on purpose to buy eggs
and butter."

"I am so sorry, I have no butter, Mr. Stumpy; but I have beautiful cauliflowers," said Robinson, lifting up the basket, after a cautious glance round at Nanny Nettigoat, who might have tried to nibble them. She was busy measuring periwinkles in a pewter mug for a duck customer in a tam-o'-shanter cap. "They are lovely brown eggs, except one that got cracked; I think that white pussy cat at the opposite stall is selling butter — they are beautiful cauliflowers."

"I'll buy a cauliflower, lovey, bless his little turned-up nose; did he grow them in his own garden?" said old Betsy, bustling up; her rheumatism was better; she had left Susan to keep house. "No, lovey, I don't want any eggs; I keep hens myself. A cauliflower and a bunch of daffodils for a bow-pot, please," said Betsy.

"WEE, wee, wee!" replied Robinson.

"Here, Mrs. Perkins, come here! Look at this little pig stuck up at a stall all by himself!"

"Well, I don't know!" exclaimed Mrs. Perkins, pushing through the crowd, followed by two little girls. "Well, I never! Are they quite new laid, sonny? Won't go off pop and spoil my Sunday dress like the eggs Mrs. Wyandotte took first prize with at five flower shows, till they popped and spoiled the judge's black silk dress? Not duck eggs, stained with coffee? That's another trick of flower shows! New laid, guaranteed? Only you say one is cracked? Now I call that real honest; it's no worse for frying. I'll have the dozen eggs and a cauliflower, please. Look, Sarah Polly! Look at his silver nose-ring."

SARAH POLLY and her little girl friend went into fits of giggling, so that Robinson blushed. He was so confused that he did not notice a lady who wanted to buy his last cauliflower, till she touched him. There was nothing else left to sell, but a bunch of primroses. After more giggling and some whispering the two little girls came back, and bought the primroses. They gave him a peppermint, as well as the penny, which Robinson accepted; but without enthusiasm and with a preoccupied manner.

The trouble was that no sooner had he parted with the bunch of primroses than he realised that he had also sold Aunt Dorcas's pattern of darning wool. He wondered if he ought to ask for it back; but Mrs. Perkins and Sarah Polly and her little girl friend had disappeared.

ROBINSON, having sold everything, came out of the market hall, sucking the peppermint. There were still numbers of people coming in. As Robinson came out upon the steps his basket got caught in the shawl of an elderly sheep, who was pushing her way up. While Robinson was disentangling it, Stumpy came out. He had finished his marketing. His basket was full of heavy purchases. A responsible, trustworthy, obliging dog was Stumpy, glad to do a kindness to anybody.

When Robinson asked him the way to Mr. Mumby's, Stumpy said: "I am going home by Broad Street. Come with me, and I will show you."

"Wee, wee, wee! Oh, thank you, Stumpy!" said Robinson.

Chapter Five

OLD Mr. Mumby was a deaf old man in spectacles, who kept a general store. He sold almost anything you can imagine, except ham — a circumstance much approved by Aunt Dorcas. It was the only general store in Stymouth where you would not find displayed upon the counter a large dish, containing strings of thin, pale-coloured, repulsively uncooked sausages, and rolled bacon hanging from the ceiling.

"WHAT pleasure," said Aunt Dorcas feelingly — "what possible pleasure can there be in entering a shop where you knock your head against a ham? A ham that may have belonged to a dear second cousin?"

Therefore the aunts bought their sugar and tea, their blue bag, their soap, their frying pans, matches, and mugs from old Mr. Mumby.

All these things he sold, and many more besides, and what he did not keep in stock he would obtain to order. But yeast requires to be quite fresh, he did not sell it; he advised Robinson to ask for yeast at a baker's shop. Also he said it was too late in the season to buy cabbage seed; everybody had finished sowing vegetable seeds this year. Worsted for darning he did sell; but Robinson had forgotten the colour.

ROBINSON bought six sticks of delightfully sticky barley sugar with his pennies, and listened carefully to Mr. Mumby's messages for Aunt Dorcas and Aunt Porcas — how they were to send some cabbages next week when the donkey cart would be mended; and how the kettle was not repaired yet, and there was a new patent box-iron he would like to recommend to Aunt Porcas.

Robinson said "Wee, wee, wee?" and listened, and little dog Tipkins who stood on a stool behind the counter, tying up grocery parcels in blue paper bags — little dog Tipkins whispered to Robinson — "Were there any rats this spring in the barn at Piggery Porcombe? And what would Robinson be doing on Saturday afternoon?"

"Wee, wee, wee!" answered Robinson.

ROBINSON came out of Mr. Mumby's, heavily laden. The barley sugar was comforting; but he was troubled about the darning wool, the yeast, and the cabbage seed. He was looking about rather anxiously, when again he met old Betsy, who exclaimed:

"Bless the little piggy! Not gone home yet? Now it must not stop in Stymouth till it gets its pocket picked!"

Robinson explained his difficulty about the darning wool.

KIND old Betsy was ready with help.

"Why, I noticed the wool round the little primrose posy; it was blue-grey colour like the last pair of socks that I knitted for Sam. Come with me to the wool shop — Fleecy Flock's wool shop. I remember the colour; well I do!" said Betsy.

Mrs. Flock was the sheep that had run against Robinson; she had bought herself three turnips and come straight home from market, for fear of missing customers while her shop was locked up.

Such a shop! Such a jumble! Wool all sorts of colours, thick wool, thin wool, fingering wool, and rug wool, bundles and bundles all jumbled up; and she could not put her hoof on anything. She was so confused and slow at finding things that Betsy got impatient.

"NO, I don't want wool for slippers; *darning wool*, Fleecy; darning wool, same colour as I bought for my Sam's socks. Bless me, *no*, not knitting needles! Darning wool."

"Baa, baa! Did you say white or black, m'm? Three ply, was it?"

"Oh, dear me, *grey* darning wool on cards; not heather mixture."

"I know I have it somewhere," said Fleecy Flock helplessly, jumbling up the skeins and bundles. "Sim Ram came in this morning with part of the Ewehampton clip; my shop is completely cluttered up —"

It took half an hour to find the wool. If Betsy had not been with him, Robinson never would have got it.

"IT'S that late, I must go home," said Betsy. "My Sam is on shore today for dinner. If you take my advice you will leave that big heavy basket with the Miss Goldfinches, and hurry with your shopping. It's a long uphill walk home to Piggery Porcombe."

Robinson, anxious to follow old Betsy's advice, walked towards the Miss Goldfinches'. On the way he came to a baker's, and he remembered the yeast.

It was not the right sort of baker's, unfortunately. There was a nice bakery smell, and pastry in the window; but it was an eating house or cook shop.

When he pushed the swing door open, a man in an apron and a square white cap turned round and said, "Hullo! Is this a pork pie walking on its hind legs?" — and four rude men at a dining table burst out laughing.

ROBINSON left the shop in a hurry. He felt afraid to go into any other baker's shop. He was looking wistfully into another window in Fore Street when Stumpy saw him again. He had taken his own basket home, and come out on another errand. He carried Robinson's basket in his mouth and took him to a very safe baker's, where he was accustomed to buy dog biscuits for himself. There Robinson purchased Aunt Dorcas's yeast at last.

They searched in vain for cabbage seed; they were told that the only likely place was a little store on the quay, kept by a pair of wagtails.

"It is a pity I cannot go with you," said Stumpy. "My Miss Rose has sprained her ankle; she sent me to fetch twelve postage stamps, and I must take them home to her, before the post goes out. Do not try to carry this heavy basket down and up the steps; leave it with the Miss Goldfinches."

ROBINSON was very grateful to Stumpy. The two Miss Goldfinches kept a tea and coffee tavern which was patronized by Aunt Dorcas and the quieter market people. Over the door was a sign board upon which was painted a fat little green bird called "The Contented Siskin", which was the name of their coffee tavern. They had a stable where the carrier's donkey rested when it came into Stymouth with the washing on Saturdays.

ROBINSON looked so tired that the elder
Miss Goldfinch gave him a cup of tea; but they
both told him to drink it up quickly.

"Wee, wee, wee! Yock yock!" said Robinson,
scalding his nose.

In spite of their respect for Aunt Dorcas, the
Miss Goldfinches disapproved of his solitary
shopping; and they said that the basket was far
too heavy for him.

"Neither of us could lift it," said the elder Miss
Goldfinch, holding out a tiny claw. "Get your
cabbage seed and hurry back. Sim Ram's pony
gig is still waiting in our stable. If you come back
before he starts I feel sure he will give you a lift;
at all events he will make room for your basket
under the seat — and he passes Piggery Porcombe.
Run away now!"

"WEE, wee, wee!" said Robinson.

"Whatever were they thinking of to let him come alone? He will never get home before dark," said the elder Miss Goldfinch. "Fly to the stable, Clara; tell Sim Ram's pony not to start without the basket."

The younger Miss Goldfinch flew across the yard. They were industrious, sprightly little lady birds, who kept lump sugar and thistle seed as well as tea in their tea-caddies. Their tables and china were spotlessly clean.

Chapter Six

STYMOUTH was full of inns; too full. The farmers usually put up their horses at the "Black Bull" or the "Horse and Farrier"; the smaller market people patronized the "Pig and Whistle".

There was another inn called the "Crown and Anchor" at the corner of Fore Street. It was much frequented by seamen; several were lounging about the door with their hands in their pockets. One sailor-man in a blue jersey sauntered across the road, staring very hard at Robinson.

Said he — "I say, little pig! do you like snuff?"

NOW if Robinson had a fault, it was that he could not say "No"; not even to a hedgehog stealing eggs. As a matter of fact, snuff or tobacco made him sick. But instead of saying, "No, thank you, Mr. Man," and going straight away about his business, he shuffled his feet, half closed one eye, hung his head on one side, and grunted.

The sailor pulled out a horn snuff box and presented a small pinch to Robinson, who wrapped it up in a little bit of paper, intending to give it to Aunt Dorcas. Then, not to be outdone in politeness, he offered the sailor-man some barley sugar.

IF Robinson was not fond of snuff, at all events his new acquaintance had no objection to candy. He ate an alarming quantity. Then he pulled Robinson's ear and complimented him, and said he had five chins. He promised to take Robinson to the cabbage seed shop; and, finally, he begged to have the honour of showing him over a ship engaged in the ginger trade, commanded by Captain Barnabas Butcher, and named the "Pound of Candles".

ROBINSON did not very much like the name. It reminded him of tallow, of lard, of crackle and trimmings of bacon. But he allowed himself to be led away, smiling shyly, and walking on his toes. If Robinson had only known . . . that man was a ship's cook!

As they turned down the steep narrow lane, out of High Street, leading to the harbour, old Mr. Mumby at his shop door called out anxiously, "Robinson! Robinson!"

BUT there was too much noise of carts. And a customer coming into the shop at that moment distracted his attention, and he forgot the suspicious behaviour of the sailor. Otherwise, out of regard for the family, he would undoubtedly have ordered his dog, Tipkins, to go and fetch Robinson back. As it was, he was the first person to give useful information to the police, when Robinson had been missed. But it was then too late.

ROBINSON and his new friend went down the long flight of steps to the harbour basin — very high steps, steep and slippery. The little pig was obliged to jump from step to step until the sailor kindly took hold of him. They walked along the quay hand in hand; their appearance seemed to cause unbounded amusement.

Robinson looked about him with much interest. He had peeped over those steps before when he had come into Stymouth in the donkey cart, but he had never ventured to go down, because the sailors are rather rough, and because they frequently have little snarling terriers on guard about their vessels.

THERE were ever so many ships in the harbour;
the noise and bustle was almost as loud as it
had been up above in the market square. A big
three-masted ship called the "Goldielocks" was
discharging a cargo of oranges; and farther along
the quay, a small coasting brig called "Little Bo
Peep" of Bristol was loading up with bales of
wool belonging to the sheep of Ewehampton
and Lambworthy.

OLD Sim Ram, with a sheepbell and big curly horns, stood by the gangway keeping count of the bales. Every time the crane swung round and let down another bale of wool into the hold, with a scuffle of rope through the pulley, Simon Ram nodded his old head, and the bell went "tinkle tinkle, tong", and he gave a gruff bleat.

He was a person who knew Robinson by sight and ought to have warned him. He had often passed Piggery Porcombe when he drove down the lane in his gig. But his blind eye was turned towards the quay; and he had been flustered and confused by an argument with the pursers as to whether thirty-five bales of wool had been hoisted on board already or only thirty-four.

SO he kept his one useful eye carefully on the wool, and counted it by the notches on his tally stick — another bale — another notch — thirty-five, thirty-six, thirty-seven; he hoped the number would come right at the finish.

His bob-tailed sheepdog, Timothy Gyp, was also acquainted with Robinson, but he was busy superintending a dog fight between an Airedale terrier belonging to the collier "Margery Dawe" and a Spanish dog belonging to the "Goldielocks". No one took any notice of their growling and snarling, which ended in both rolling over the side of the quay and falling into the water. Robinson kept close to the sailor and held his hand very tight.

The "Pound of Candles" proved to be a good-sized schooner, newly painted and decorated with certain flags, whose significance was not understood by Robinson. She lay near the outer end of the jetty.

THE tide was running up fast, lapping against the ship's sides and straining the thick hawsers by which she was moored to the quay.

The crew were stowing goods on board and doing things with ropes under the direction of Captain Barnabas Butcher; a lean, brown, nautical person with a rasping voice. He banged things about and grumbled; parts of his remarks were audible on the quay. He was speaking about the tug "Sea-horse" — and about the spring tide, with a north-east wind behind it — and the baker's man and fresh vegetables — "to be shipped at eleven sharp; likewise a joint of . . ." He stopped short suddenly, and his eye lighted upon the cook and Robinson.

ROBINSON and the cook went on board across a shaky plank. When Robinson stepped on to the deck, he found himself face to face with a large yellow cat who was blacking boots.

The cat gave a start of surprise and dropped its blacking brush. It then began to wink and make extraordinary faces at Robinson. He had never seen a cat behave in that way before. He inquired whether it was ill. Whereupon the cook threw a boot at it, and it rushed up into the rigging. But Robinson he invited most affably to descend into the cabin, to partake of muffins and crumpets.

I do not know how many muffins Robinson consumed. He went on eating them until he fell asleep; and he went on sleeping until his stool gave a lurch, and he fell off and rolled under the table. One side of the cabin floor swung up to the ceiling; and the other side of the ceiling swung down to the floor. Plates danced about; and there were shoutings and thumpings and rattling of chains and other bad sounds.

Robinson picked himself up, feeling bumped. He scrambled up a sort of a ladder-staircase on to the deck. Then he gave squeal upon squeal of horror! All round the ship there were great big green waves; the houses on the quay were like dolls' houses; and high up inland, above the red cliffs and green fields, he could see the farm of Piggery Porcombe looking no bigger than a postage stamp.

A little white patch in the orchard was Aunt Porcas's washing, spread out to bleach upon the grass. Near at hand the black tug "Sea-horse" smoked and plunged and rolled. They were winding in the tow rope which had just been cast loose from the "Pound of Candles".

CAPTAIN BARNABAS stood up in the bows of his schooner; he yelled and shouted to the master of the tug. The sailors shouted also, and pulled with a will, and hoisted the sails. The ship heeled over and rushed through the waves, and there was a smell of the sea.

As for Robinson — he tore round and round the deck like one distracted, shrieking very shrill and loud. Once or twice he slipped down; for the deck was extremely sideways; but still he ran and he ran. Gradually his squeals subsided into singing, but still he kept on running, and this is what he sang —

"Poor Pig Robinson Crusoe!
Oh, how in the world could they do so?
They have set him afloat, in a horrible boat,
Oh, poor pig Robinson Crusoe!"

THE sailors laughed until they cried; but when Robinson had sung that same verse about fifty times, and upset several sailors by rushing between their legs, they began to get angry. Even the ship's cook was no longer civil to Robinson. On the contrary, he was very rude indeed. He said that if Robinson did not leave off singing through his nose, he would make him into pork chops.

Then Robinson fainted, and fell flat upon the deck of the "Pound of Candles".

Chapter Seven

IT must not be supposed for one moment that Robinson was ill-treated on board ship. Quite the contrary. He was even better fed and more petted on the "Pound of Candles" than he had been at Piggery Porcombe. So, after a few days' fretting for his kind old aunts (especially while he was seasick), Robinson became perfectly contented and happy. He found what is called his "sea legs"; and he scampered about the deck until the time when he became too fat and lazy to scamper.

THE cook was never tired of boiling porridge
for him. A whole sack full of meal and a sack of
potatoes appeared to have been provided especially
for his benefit and pleasure. He could eat as much
as he pleased. It pleased him to eat a great deal
and to lie on the warm boards of the deck. He
got lazier and lazier as the ship sailed south into
warmer weather. The mate made a pet of him; the
crew gave him tit-bits. The cook rubbed his back
and scratched his sides — his ribs could not be
tickled, because he had laid so much fat on.
The only persons who refused to treat him as
a joke were the yellow tom-cat and Captain
Barnabas Butcher, who was of a sour disposition.

THE attitude of the cat was perplexing to Robinson. Obviously it disapproved of the maize meal porridge business, and it spoke mysteriously about the impropriety of greediness, and about the disastrous results of over-indulgence. But it did not explain what those results might be, and as the cat itself cared neither for yellow meal nor 'taties, Robinson thought that its warnings might arise from prejudice. It was not unfriendly. It was mournful and foreboding.

The cat itself was crossed in love. Its morose and gloomy outlook upon life was partly the result of separation from the owl. That sweet hen-bird, a snowy owl of Lapland, had sailed upon a northern whaler, bound for Greenland. Whereas the "Pound of Candles" was heading for the tropic seas.

THEREFORE the cat neglected its duties, and was upon the worst of terms with the cook. Instead of blacking boots and valeting the Captain, it spent days and nights in the rigging, serenading the moon. Between times it came down on deck, and remonstrated with Robinson.

It never told him plainly why he ought not to eat so much; but it referred frequently to a mysterious date (which Robinson could never remember) — the date of Captain Butcher's birthday, which he celebrated annually by an extra good dinner.

"That's what they are saving up apples for. The onions are done — sprouted with the heat. I heard Captain Barnabas tell the cook that onions were of no consequence as long as there were apples for sauce."

ROBINSON paid no attention. In fact, he and the cat were both on the side of the ship, watching a shoal of silvery fishes. The ship was completely becalmed. The cook strolled across the deck to see what the cat was looking at and exclaimed joyfully at sight of fresh fish. Presently half the crew were fishing. They baited their lines with bits of scarlet wool and bits of biscuit; and the boatswain had a successful catch on a line baited with a shiny button.

The worst of button fishing was that so many fish dropped off while being hauled on deck. Consequently Captain Butcher allowed the crew to launch the jolly boat, which was let down from some iron contraption called "the davits" on to the glassy surface of the sea. Five sailors got into the boat; the cat jumped in also. They fished for hours. There was not a breath of wind.

IN the absence of the cat, Robinson fell asleep peacefully upon the warm deck. Later he was disturbed by the voices of the mate and the cook, who had not gone fishing. The former was saying:

"I don't fancy loin of pork with sun-stroke, Cooky. Stir him up; or else throw a piece of sail cloth over him. I was bred on a farm myself. Pigs should never be let sleep in a hot sun."

"As why?" inquired the cook.

"Sunstroke," replied the mate. "Likewise it scorches the skin; makes it peely like; spoils the look of the crackling."

At this point a rather heavy dirty piece of sail cloth was flung over Robinson, who struggled and kicked with sudden grunts.

"DID he hear you, Matey?" asked the cook in a lower voice.

"Don't know; don't matter; he can't get off the ship," replied the mate, lighting his pipe.

"Might upset his appetite; he's feeding beautiful," said the cook.

Presently the voice of Captain Barnabas Butcher was heard. He had come up on deck after a siesta below in his cabin.

"Proceed to the crow's nest on the main mast; observe the horizon through a telescope according to latitude and longitude. We ought to be amongst the archipelago by the chart and compass," said the voice of Captain Butcher.

It reached the ears of Robinson through the sail cloth in muffled tones, but peremptory; although it was not so received by the mate, who occasionally contradicted the Captain when no one else was listening.

"MY corns are very painful," said the mate.

"Send the cat up," ordered Captain Barnabas briefly.

"The cat is out in the boat fishing."

"Fetch him in then," said Captain Barnabas, losing his temper. "He has not blacked my boots for a fortnight." He went below; that is, down a step-ladder into his cabin, where he proceeded to work out the latitude and longitude again, in search of the archipelago.

"It's to be hoped that he mends his temper before next Thursday, or he won't enjoy roast pork!" said the mate to the cook.

They strolled to the other end of the deck to see what fish had been caught; the boat was coming back.

AS the weather was perfectly calm, it was left over night upon the glassy sea, tied below a port-hole (or ship's window) at the stern of the "Pound of Candles".

The cat was sent up the mast with a telescope; it remained there for some time. When it came down it reported quite untruthfully that there was nothing in sight. No particular watch or look-out was kept that night upon the "Pound of Candles" because the ocean was so calm. The cat was supposed to watch — if anybody did. All the rest of the ship's company played cards.

Not so the cat or Robinson. The cat had noticed a slight movement under the sail cloth. It found Robinson shivering with fright and in floods of tears. He had overheard the conversation about pork.

"I'M sure I have given you enough hints," said the cat to Robinson. "What do you suppose they were feeding you up for? Now don't start squealing, you little fool! It's as easy as snuff, if you will listen and stop crying. You can row, after a fashion." (Robinson had been out fishing occasionally and caught several crabs.) "Well, you have not far to go; I could see the top of the Bong tree on an island N.N.E., when I was up the mast. The straits of the archipelago are too shallow for the "Pound of Candles", and I'll scuttle all the other boats. Come along, and do what I tell you!" said the cat.

THE cat, actuated partly by unselfish friendship, and partly by a grudge against the cook and Captain Barnabas Butcher, assisted Robinson to collect a varied assortment of necessaries. Shoes, sealing-wax, a knife, an armchair, fishing tackle, a straw hat, a saw, fly papers, a potato pot, a telescope, a kettle, a compass, a hammer, a barrel of flour, another of meal, a keg of fresh water, a tumbler, a teapot, nails, a bucket, a screwdriver—

"That reminds me," said the cat, and what did it do but go round the deck with a gimlet and bore large holes in the three boats that remained on board the "Pound of Candles".

BY this time there began to be ominous sounds below; those of the sailors who had had bad hands were beginning to be tired of carding. So the cat took a hasty farewell of Robinson, pushed him over the ship's side, and he slid down the rope into the boat. The cat unfastened the upper end of the rope and threw it after him. Then it ascended the rigging and pretended to sleep upon its watch.

Robinson stumbled somewhat in taking his seat at the oars. His legs were short for rowing. Captain Barnabas in the cabin suspended his deal, a card in his hand, listening (the cook took the opportunity to look under the card), then he went on slapping down the cards, which drowned the sound of oars upon the placid sea.

AFTER another hand, two sailors left the cabin and went on deck. They noticed something having the appearance of a large black beetle in the distance. One of them said it was an enormous cockroach, swimming with its hind legs. The other said it was a dolphinium. They disputed, rather loudly. Captain Barnabas, who had had a hand with no trumps at all after the cook dealing — Captain Barnabas came on deck and said:

"Bring me my telescope."

The telescope had disappeared; likewise the shoes, the sealing-wax, the compass, the potato pot, the straw hat, the hammer, the nails, the bucket, the screwdriver, and the armchair.

"Take the jolly boat and see what it is," ordered Captain Butcher.

"All jolly fine, but suppose it is a dolphinium?" said the mate mutinously.

"WHY, bless my life, the jolly boat is gone!" exclaimed a sailor.

"Take another boat, take all the three other boats; it's that pig and that cat!" roared the Captain.

"NAY, sir, the cat's up the rigging asleep."

"Bother the cat! Get the pig back! The apple sauce will be wasted!" shrieked the cook, dancing about and brandishing a knife and fork.

The davits were swung out, the boats were let down with a swish and a splash, all the sailors tumbled in, and rowed frantically. And most of them were glad to row frantically back to the "Pound of Candles". For every boat leaked badly, thanks to the cat.

Chapter Eight

ROBINSON rowed away from the "Pound of Candles". He tugged steadily at the oars. They were heavy for him. The sun had set, but I understand that in the tropics — I have never been there — there is a phosphorescent light upon the sea. When Robinson lifted his oars, the sparkling water dripped from the blades like diamonds. And presently the moon began to rise above the horizon — rising like half a great silver plate.

ROBINSON rested on his oars and gazed at the ship, motionless in the moonlight, on a sea without a ripple. It was at this moment — he being a quarter of a mile away — that the two sailors came on deck, and thought his boat was a swimming beetle.

Robinson was too far away to see or hear the uproar on board the "Pound of Candles"; but he did presently perceive that three boats were starting in pursuit. Involuntarily he commenced to squeal, and rowed frantically. But before he had time to exhaust himself by racing, the ship's boats turned back. Then Robinson remembered the cat's work with the gimlet, and he knew that the boats were leaking.

FOR the rest of the night he rowed quietly, without haste. He was not inclined to sleep, and the air was pleasantly cool. Next day it was hot, but Robinson slept soundly under the sail cloth, which the cat had been careful to send with him, in case he wished to rig up a tent.

THE ship receded from view — you know the sea is not really flat. First he could not see the hull, then he could not see the deck, then only part of the masts, then nothing at all.

Robinson had been steering his course by the ship. Having lost sight of this direction sign, he turned round to consult his compass — when bump, bump, the boat touched a sandbank. Fortunately it did not stick.

Robinson stood up in the boat, working one oar backwards, and gazing around. What should he see but the top of the Bong tree!

Half an hour's rowing brought him to the beach of a large and fertile island. He landed in the most approved manner in a convenient sheltered bay, where a stream of boiling water flowed down the silvery strand. The shore was covered with oysters. Acid drops and sweets grew upon the trees.

YAMS, which are a sort of sweet potato, abounded ready cooked. The bread-fruit tree grew iced cakes and muffins, ready baked; so no pig need sigh for porridge. Overhead towered the Bong tree.

IF you want a more detailed description of the island, you must read "Robinson Crusoe". The island of the Bong tree was very like Crusoe's, only without its drawbacks. I have never been there myself, so I rely upon the report of the Owl and the Pussy Cat, who visited it eighteen months later, and spent a delightful honeymoon there. They spoke enthusiastically about the climate — only it was a little too warm for the Owl.

Later on Robinson was visited by Stumpy and little dog Tipkins. They found him perfectly contented, and in the best of good health. He was not at all inclined to return to Stymouth. For anything I know he may be living there still upon the island. He grew fatter and fatter and more fatterer; and the ship's cook never found him.

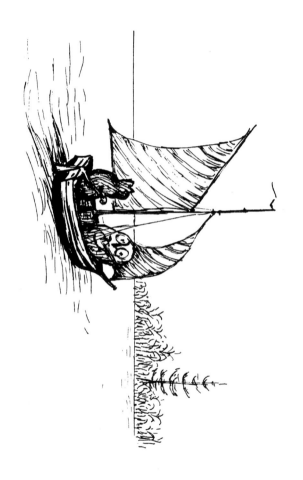